Sue Patch
and the Crazy Clocks

Ann Tompert

PICTURES BY

Rosekrans Hoffman

DIAL BOOKS FOR YOUNG READERS · New York

Published by Dial Books for Young Readers
A Division of Penguin Books USA Inc.
2 Park Avenue
New York, New York 10016

Published simultaneously in Canada by
Fitzhenry & Whiteside Limited, Toronto

Library of Congress Cataloging in Publication Data
Tompert, Ann. Sue Patch and the crazy clocks
by Ann Tompert; pictures by Rosekrans Hoffman.
p. cm.
Summary: The King of Tango appeals to Sue Patch,
who can fix anything, because all the clocks in his palace
are set at different times and he cannot function in
the resulting chaos.
ISBN 0-8037-0656-1. ISBN 0-8037-0658-8 (lib. bdg.)
[1. Clocks and watches—Fiction.
2. Kings, queens, rulers, etc.—Fiction.]
I. Hoffman, Rosekrans, ill. II. Title.
PZ7.T598Su 1989 [E]—dc19 88-25720 CIP AC

First Edition
W
1 3 5 7 9 10 8 6 4 2

The full-color artwork was prepared using pencil,
colored pencils, and colored inks.
It was then color-separated and reproduced
as red, blue, yellow, and black halftones.

Reading Level 2.5

For Bob
A.T.

For James Charles and Jessie
R.H.

Sue Patch was a handy person.

She could fix anything.

She liked to help

the people who lived

in the kingdom of Tango

by fixing

bent keys,

hurt knees,

doors that creaked,

roofs that leaked,

leaning towers,

wilting flowers,

torn books,

unhappy looks,

and anything else

that needed fixing.

One day the King of Tango
called her on the telephone.
"My clocks have gone crazy,"
he said. "Will you help me?"

"Right away," said Sue Patch.
She put on her pinwheel hat,
picked up her bag of tricks,
and climbed to the roof
of her house.

Up, up, up

into the sky

she flew.

When she got to

the King of Tango's palace,

the King was waiting outside.

He waved her

to a safe landing.

Then he clapped his hands.

A footman ran to them.

"What time is it?"

asked the King.

"Three o'clock,"

answered the footman.

"Time to count my gold,"
cried the King.
"On to the counting room."
He ran toward the palace.
Sue Patch ran after him.
Up, up, up they climbed—
one set of stairs,
two sets of stairs,
three, four, five
sets of stairs,
six, seven, eight, nine, ten
sets of stairs—
to reach the counting room
in the palace tower.

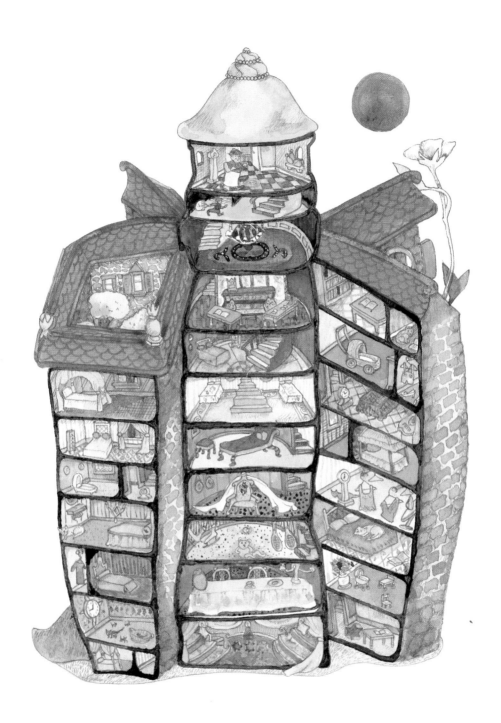

13

BONG! BONG! BONG! BONG! BONG!

rang the grandfather clock

as they went

into the counting room.

"It can't be five o'clock
so soon!" exclaimed Sue Patch.
"It was only three o'clock
when I came."

"If it's five o'clock,

I should be

in the great hall,"

cried the King.

"It's time to meet the toymakers."

Down, down, down

they flew—

one set of stairs,

two sets of stairs,

three, four, five

sets of stairs,

six, seven, eight, nine, ten

sets of stairs—

to the great hall.

But when they got there,

they found no toymakers.

"They have gone already,"

said a footman.

DING! DING! DING! DING!

rang the banjo clock

on the wall.

"Four o'clock!" cried the King.

"Time for tea!

I don't want to miss that."

The King dashed off

to the dining hall

with Sue Patch on his heels.

In the dining hall they found

a table loaded

with good things to eat.

"Help yourself," said the King.

"I'm having a jelly roll."

"Me too," said Sue Patch.

As she picked up

the jelly roll,

the clock on the mantel rang.

CLANG! CLANG!

Three footmen came

and rolled the table away.

"Wait," cried Sue Patch.

"Can't wait,"

said the first footman.

"Two o'clock is

too late for lunch,"

said the second footman.

"And it's too early for tea,"

said the third footman.

"Time to read,"

said the King.

He ran out of the room

with Sue Patch on his heels.

23

When they got to the reading room,

the King sank into a chair.

"I'm worn out," he said.

Sue Patch sank into another chair.

"So am I," she said.

A clock on a shelf rang

ten o'clock.

"Time for bed," said the King.

"Your clocks *are* crazy,"

said Sue Patch.

"Can you fix them?" asked the King.

"Easy as pie," said Sue Patch,

snapping her fingers.

"Have all the clocks

moved into one room.

Then we'll set them all

at the same time."

"We can't move the clocks,"

said the King.

"It's against the law.

My great, great, great

grandfather wrote the law,

and I can't bear to change it."

"No problem," said Sue Patch.
"What time would you
like it to be right now?"

"Six o'clock," said the King.
"That's when we have dinner,
and I'm hungry
after all that running."

"Me too," said Sue Patch.
She climbed on a chair
and set the clock on the shelf
at six o'clock.

"Now send your fastest footman
to set the rest of the clocks
at six o'clock," she said.

The fastest footman
set the clock in the great hall
at six o'clock.

He set the clock in the throne room
at six o'clock.

He set the clock in the game room
at six o'clock.

The clocks in the hundred bedrooms
and the writing room
were set at six.

So was the ballroom clock.

The fastest footman raced
round and round the palace
setting all the clocks at six.

It took him five hours

to reach the counting room

at the top

of the palace.

He set its clock at six.

When he was done,

there still were

no two palace clocks

that told the same time.

The throne room clock

rang nine

at the same time that

the great hall clock

rang eleven.

"My clocks are still crazy,"
said the King.
"I'll try something else,"
said Sue Patch.

"What time do you like best
in the morning?" she asked.
"Seven o'clock," said the King.
"That's breakfast time."
"Seven o'clock it will be,"
said Sue Patch.

She sent a footman

to stand by each clock

in the palace.

Then she set the clock

in the great hall at seven.

"It's seven o'clock and

all is well," she yelled

as loudly as she could.

But the words got muddled

as they floated

around the palace.

The footman

in the dining hall heard,

"It's eleven o'clock

so ring the bell."

He set his clock at eleven.

The footman

in the reading room heard,

"Ten o'clock is the time I tell."

He set his clock at ten.

All the other

footmen heard

different numbers

and set their clocks

at different times.

The footman

in the counting room

at the top

of the palace

didn't hear anything at all,

so he took the hands off

the grandfather clock.

"Fixing your clocks

will be harder

than I thought,"

said Sue Patch,

searching in her bag of tricks.

"Can't you do it?"

asked the King.

"I haven't failed yet,"
said Sue Patch.
She took off her hat,
rolled up her sleeves,
and searched in her bag
of tricks some more.

"I have it," she said,

holding up a gold beaded cord.

"How will that help me?"

asked the King.

"You'll see," said Sue Patch.

And she sent
all the King's footmen
to hunt for the smallest clock
in the palace.

Then Sue Patch said,
"Are you the King of Tango?"
"Of course," said the King.
"Everyone knows that."

"You have the King's palace,"
said Sue Patch.

"Yes, yes," said the King.

"You have the King's horses,
the King's men, the King's robes,
and the King's crown,"
she said.

"Yes, yes," said the King.

"Then you should have
the King's clock,"
she said.

She put the clock on the cord
and slipped it
around the King's neck.

"How jolly!" exclaimed the King.

"Now wherever I go

I'll carry the time with me."

"And you'll always be on time,"

said Sue Patch.

The King wound the clock.

"What time is it?" he asked.

"Time?" said Sue Patch.

"Why, it's time for me to go."

She put on her pinwheel hat,

grabbed her bag of tricks,

and climbed to the roof

of the palace.

Up, up, up into the sky
she went.

And she sailed for home.